A-Hunting We Will Go!

A-Hunting We Will Go!

STEVEN KELLOGG

HarperCollins*Publishers*

A combination of colored ink, watercolor, acrylic,
and colored pencil was used for the full-color illustrations.
The text type is 26-point Zapf International Light.

A-Hunting We Will Go!
Copyright © 1998 by Steven Kellogg

Library of Congress Cataloging-in-Publication Data
Kellogg, Steven.
A-hunting we will go! / Steven Kellogg.
p.   cm.
Summary: In this modern version of the children's song, preparations for bedtime
include "A-reading we will go! Now to the bath we go! Now off to bed we go!"
ISBN 0-688-14944-8 (trade)—ISBN 0-688-14945-6 (library)—ISBN 0-06-443747-7 (pbk.)
1. Children's songs—Texts. [1. Hunting—Songs and music.
2. Bedtime—Songs and music. 3. Songs.] I. Title.
PZ8.3.K33Aae 1998 782.42164'0268—
dc21clopedias. [E] 97-47296
CIP AC

❖

Visit us on the World Wide Web!
www.harperchildrens.com

A-HUNTING WE WILL GO!

A-hunting we will go!
Our hunting horn we'll BLOW!

The bears in front will lead the hunt,

A-hunting we will go! A-hunting we will go!
Moose and Goose are on the loose.

A-hunting we will go! A-hunting we will go!
Get that weasel at the easel.

A-hunting we will go! A-hunting we will go!
We'll tickle a giraffe and make him laugh.

A-hunting we will go! A-hunting we will go!
Behind the door

or in a drawer, you'll find

A-hunting we will go! A-hunting we will go!
We'll catch a kangaroo,

or TWO!

Then hop aboard

And ROW, and...

A-reading we will go! A-reading we will go!

A pod of whales will love our tales,

So Dale the whale survived the gale while Mark the shark was sent to jail.

The End

And
then
they'll
dive
below!

Now to the bath we go! The faucets soon will flow!

Moose gets tubbed,

And Goose gets scrubbed.

They'll
glow
from
head
to toe!

A-brushing we will go! A-brushing we will go!

Will the polars brush their molars?

YES,
YES,
YES,
YES,

Pajamming we will go! Pajamming we will go!

Put the llamas in pajamas.

Find the fox a pair of socks.

Give each bear clean underwear.

Then, with our friends in tow...

A-hugging we will go! A-hugging we will go!
We'll find our parents, hug them tight.

We'll snuggle up and say good night

Because we love them so!

Now off to bed we go! Yes, off to bed we go!

Our hunting ends, our hugging ends.

But we'll be joined by all our friends,

And off to sleep

we'll
go.

Author's Note

The folk song "A-Hunting We Will Go" has existed for over three hundred years. It has been associated with several different tunes—some of which have blended with similar songs, including "The Farmer in the Dell"—as well as a variety of line and ring dances, "grab" games, double-rank dances, and kissing games. It is thought to have originated in the 1600s as an English country dance, eventually evolving into a game in which children form two parallel rows. Each facing pair in turn holds hands and skips down the middle to rhythmic clapping; the pair at the top then goes around the outside and makes an archway with their arms, under which the others pass.

Another version of the dance is related to the fox-hunting games from English folklore, where one dancer acts as the "fox," being chased and captured by the "hunter," thus illustrating the original lyrics to the song:

A-hunting we will go! A-hunting we will go!
We'll catch a fox and put him in a box and never let him go!

Part of the tradition of "A-Hunting We Will Go" has been to encourage participants to create their own verses during the course of the game. In this book, I have written new words for the familiar tune, recasting the hunting of animals as a roundup of congenial beasts who join two children on a playful journey toward bedtime.

A-Hunting We Will Go!

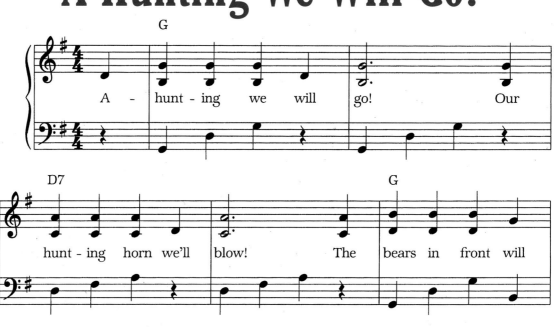

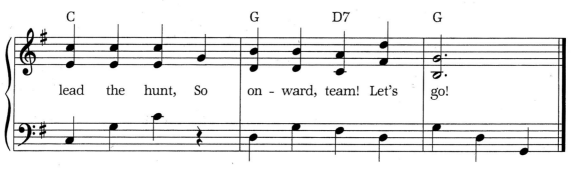